Macmillan Publishing Co., Inc., 866 Third Avenue, New York, N.Y. 10022. Collier Macmillan Canada, Ltd. Printed in the United States of America. *Library of Congress Cataloging in Publication Data:* Berson, Harold. Truffles for lunch. *Summary:* A wizard grants a pig's wish to be another animal, but it proves to be distressingly unsatisfactory. [1. Pigs—Fiction. 2. Animals—Fiction. 3. Wishes—Fiction] I. Title. PZ7.B4623Tr 1980 [E] 80-13367 ISBN 0-02-709800-1. 10 9 8 7 6 5 4 3 2 1

TRUFFLES FOR LUNCH

BY HAROLD BERSON

MACMILLAN PUBLISHING CO., INC.
New York
COLLIER MACMILLAN PUBLISHERS
London

Phil was unhappy. "Oh, to have a beautiful voice that could wake up everyone in the morning," he said to the rooster. "How nice that would be."

"Or a nice, warm, curly wool coat. That would be just the thing for winter," he said to the sheep, looking at his own short bristles.

"A fine, feathery, spreading tail would be spectacular," he thought as the turkey pranced by.

And as the bull charged off across the barnyard, Phil called, "Your horns! Ah, they're magnificent!"

Finally, to the horse he said, "How lucky you are to have such long, strong legs. To run free over the fields of grass and flowers. Oh my!"

Phil's friends told him not to worry so much. He was just fine the way he was. But Phil didn't believe them. Not one bit. And he decided to leave home.

As Phil slowly walked down the road away from the farm, he thought about where to go and what to do once he got there. Suddenly, just ahead, he spotted a large circus poster nailed to a tree. "Ah," said Phil to no one in particular. "To be a lion. To be fearless, strong, handsome, and brave. To be the King of Beasts! Ah, that would be the life." And he walked on into the forest.

Before he had gone very far, Phil heard laughter.
"Ho, ho! What's this?" laughed the wolf. "Whatever it is, it doesn't have any fangs."

"And where's his fur?" laughed the fox.

"He's so small," roared the bear.

"And so smooth," snickered the porcupine.

"Look at that tail! Couldn't use that for hanging upside down," said the possum.

Then the snake, noting that he too lacked most of these fine things, quickly chimed in, "And no nice designs, either. Not a one to be seen. Goodness."

Phil ran deeper into the woods, unhappier than ever.

Soon it was noon, and Phil decided to rest under a tree to eat lunch and make plans. As he sat there munching berries and relaxing, he heard a commotion above him.

"Hey! Up here. Hey! Can you give me a hand? I'm The Wizard of the Woods and the Streams and Everything Else Around Here. I've really fouled things up this time, though. My flying instinct must be off, or something. Anyway, now I'm up here and my magic hat is down there. And I can't do a thing without it. Say, little fellow, can you get my hat up to me?"

"Gee," answered Phil, "I'll try. But I'm not too good at climbing trees. And I'm not too terrific at throwing things, either. Let me think." Phil thought and thought and then he said, "I've got it!" He placed a stick over a stone, carefully laid the Wizard's hat on one end, balancing it just so, and with a running jump landed on the other end. Up flew the magic hat, right into the hands of the stranded Wizard.

"Thank you, sir. Thank you," said the Wizard as he swooped down and landed beside Phil. "Name it. Any wish you name is yours."

Without a moment's hesitation, Phil said, "I want to be a lion."

The Wizard threw up his arms. Phil the pig whirled into a cloud of dust and Phil the lion stepped out.

"You're a lion," said the Wizard. And off he flew.

"Ah, how strong I am!"

"What fantastic fur!"

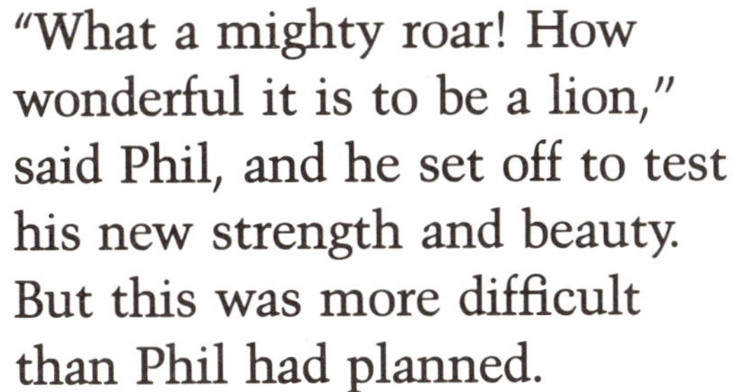

"What a mighty roar! How wonderful it is to be a lion," said Phil, and he set off to test his new strength and beauty. But this was more difficult than Phil had planned.

Now everyone was afraid of him, and he couldn't even get close enough for them to admire his wonderful fur, feel his strong muscles, or hear his mighty roar. Even worse, he was getting hungry and wasn't too certain about how to go about getting lion food. "Well," he thought, "the first beast I meet, I eat."

Easier said than done.
The fox was much too clever.
The possum was much too high.

The porcupine was much too prickly.

And to make things even more difficult, the hot noon sun was making all of that new fur terribly itchy and scratchy.

Phil began to think of his former life as a pig. "Ah," he thought, "how nice it was back on the farm, rolling about in the nice cool mud."

"And how nice it was to eat whenever and whatever I wanted. Well, I'll just have to learn how to hunt."

And he started off again down the road. Turning a corner, he bumped into a little pig.

"Oops," squealed the pig.

Turning on her heel, she ran off as fast as she could, followed by the bounding, snarling Phil. She dodged this way and that and ran just as fast as she could. Soon her heart was pounding like a drum.

Then she fell to the ground, her legs unable to move. She shut her eyes tightly and waited for the end. "It's all over for me," she whispered to herself. "Alas, how short life is."

But nothing happened. Fearfully, the little pig opened one eye.

"Aren't you going to eat me?" she said in a tiny voice.

"I can't," sobbed Phil, large tears pouring down his mane.

"You can't?" squeaked the pig, hopefully.

"No, I can't. I used to be a pig myself, you see, until The Wizard of the Woods changed me into a lion. Now I'm King of Beasts, but it isn't doing me much good. Everyone's afraid of me. My fur itches. I'm hungry and I can't find a thing to eat. And, now that I've finally caught something, I can't go through with eating it."

"Oh," said the little pig, not believing a word of this. "Look, call me Lucy. I'll think of something. Um… why don't you try eating a few truffles? They're sort of like mushrooms and my very favorite food. I bet I can find some for you." And she quickly began to dig.

"Ugh," cried Phil, biting into a truffle. "These are terrible!" And he spat them out.

"How about some berries," said Lucy. And she ran into the bushes to find some.

"Worse!" roared Phil.

"Perhaps corn?" whispered Lucy. "A farm is close by here. Come on, I'll show you the way."

But Phil was getting weak from hunger. "I've got to rest," he said, collapsing underneath a huge tree. "Maybe after a short nap I'll have the nerve to eat this charming creature," he thought.

And he tied Lucy to the tree and dozed off.

He awoke to twigs and leaves falling on his nose. He looked up into the tree, and there sat The Wizard of the Woods.

"Well, hello, hello, hello," said the Wizard. "I guess I've done it again, haven't I? Would you mind doing me another favor and kindly toss up my magic hat?"

"I sure will," said Phil. "And I'll bet that you can give wishes back."

"Yes, indeed," said the Wizard. "What's the problem?"

"Well, I'm tired of being a lion. And hungry, too. Now I want to be...."

"To be a pig again," finished the Wizard. "I know."

And he waved his arms.
Phil the lion whirled into a cloud
of dust and Phil the pig
stepped out.

"Gee, you really weren't kidding," said Lucy as Phil untied her from the tree.

"No," said Phil. "And I wasn't kidding about being hot and hungry, either."

"Good," said Lucy. "I just happen to know a nice cool spot where there's a large patch of truffles." And they walked off happily together to have a pig's favorite lunch.